WARNING

This book contains sexually explicit scenes and adult language. It may be considered offensive to some readers. This book is for sale to adults ONLY.

* * * * * * * * * * * * * * * *

Please store your files wisely where they cannot be accessed by underage readers.

ISBN-13: 978-1987863444
ISBN-10: 1987863445

Other books by Shyla Starr:

<u>Persuasive Billionaire BWWM Romance Series</u>

Stacey is trying to keep a handle on her life the best that she can. She is on the verge of losing her job and her apartment, while taking care of her sick grandmother. Her life takes an unexpected turn when she meets Charlie, who works for the construction company that is attempting to persuade her to move out of her home.

<u>Tenacious Billionaire BWWM Romance Series</u>

Adalia is too proud to accept help from the billionaire playboy, Trent Dawson. How long can she maintain her resolve? The bank is at her heels to repossess her business. To make matters worse, Adalia finds suspicious evidence of Trent's philandering ways. She must determine whether to trust Trent with the fate of her business and her heart.

<u>Lonely Billionaire Romance Series</u>

Tricia was hired to care for billionaire John's wife, who is dying. An unlikely romance emerges after his wife, Rebecca, gives John permission to pursue his happiness after she is gone.

<u>Ardent Billionaire Romance Series</u>

Deirdre doesn't know what to make of the gorgeous man that seems to be interested in her. His name is Parker Walters and he seems friendly enough. There is just something off about him. Why is he trying the hide the fact that he is the heir to his father's billion dollar software empire?

Fervent Billionaire BWWM Romance Series

Alexandra had never been with a white man before. She had seen William at the café before but she always kept her distance. It was unfortunate that their first chance meeting happened when she dropped her breakfast and spilled coffee all over his expensive business suit.

Audacious Billionaire BWWM Romance Series

Chante is torn between staying close to a man beyond her league, and fleeing from him to spare herself from a hopeless position. But she finds she is propelled into a place where she needs to confront her doubts and cast her fate aside to follow the dictates of her heart. Damned if she does and miserable is she doesn't, how will Chante face the events that will lead her to a place of pure happiness or to the pits of a broken heart?

Get the latest update on new releases from the author at:

https://shylastarr.com/newsletter/

This book is Part One of the "Elusive Billionaire Romance Series"

1 - Suspicion

Billionaire Hendrick is trying to repair his company's image by putting in some volunteer work, building a school and hospital for the impoverished children in Africa. There, he meets a beautiful African American volunteer, Jocelyn. They hit it off right away but does she belong in his world?

2 - Love Belated

What had Jocelyn done? Why was she being a fool by falling in love so soon? Not trusting her feelings, Jocelyn decided to return home and immerse herself in her work. Perhaps if she kept busy and dated other men, she can forget Hendrick. Things seemed to be going well and a wedding date with her man, Tim, was set. Nothing was going to ruin her day...until a man she was trying to forget shows up the night before the wedding.

3 - Love Amiss

Finally, Jocelyn started her new life with her chosen man. Was it the right decision? At one point or another, she was in love with either Tim or Hendrick. How could that be? The birth of her daughter, Jasmine, was supposed to ground and solidify her marriage. Instead, her partner's jealousy over her past relationship loomed overhead like a dark cloud.

Elusive Billionaire Romance Series

Suspicion

Book One

By Shyla Starr

Copyright Revelry Publishing 2015

Table of Contents

Chapter One

"**I WANT** to know who the hell is responsible for this mess!" boomed Hendrick from the front of the boardroom.

Silence filled the room as all the top people in the company stared at Hendrick in awe. They knew he wasn't the kind of guy to be messed with. Considering the company had just been charged with federal and criminal charges for dumping industrial waste into the Arctic Ocean, they knew it was best to stay silent.

"I return from vacation to find the prosecutor in my office to tell me that a company that I built from the ground up to help humanity is being accused of filling the ocean with waste! Waste??" He screamed across the table, his face turning an angry red. Hendrick stopped for a moment to compose himself and looked at each person at the table, assessing their worth.

"Pray it was not one of you frontrunners that made the decision to handle the waste of the company in this manner. Now go, and I expect reports hourly about how we are making this right and where waste should be going from now on."

Everyone got up from the table quickly and filtered out of the room. Hendrick watched them all leave and turned to his right-hand man, Geoffrey, the CEO of the company.

"Tell me you didn't know."

A broad-shouldered man, Geoffrey held an imposing frame that fit well with the red beard that made him appear like a Viking. He was incredibly loyal and a great asset to the company.

"You have known me your whole life Hendrick, I'm sure you know I had nothing to do with dumping waste into the ocean. The person in charge of a decision like that is one of your minions."

"How is it that the owner and CEO of a company had no idea that his own company has been poisoning the ocean?"

"Someone down the line obviously felt it would save the company a lot of money."

Hendrick snorted, "Ya and no one would ever find out that the Arctic Ocean was suddenly polluted? My god they have vessel numbers and everything, it was our guys to be sure, so how do I not know about it?"

"The prosecutors are doing their investigation and so are we. I can guarantee that we will find out who is responsible before anyone else does."

"I'm being prosecuted, Geoffrey! They think I knew about this madness."

"Look you didn't know and they can't prove that you did. You will have your day in court and they will simply have to let it go. They can't pull evidence from thin air so you're safe."

Hendrick went to the side table by the grand picture window. He poured them both a glass of bourbon, handing one to Geoffrey.

"I built this company because I believed in a vision and now our reputation is being smeared. All the while I'm off doing fundraisers and charity events while some asshole is destroying the ocean under my name."

"Hendrick, it's your job to do those things. That's how money is raised and you don't need to be at the company all the time, that's my job, to handle the bullshit. I apologize that this issue slipped through my fingers. I assure you it will be handled, we certainly won't be dealing with such an issue as this in the future."

They clinked glasses before Hendrick took a strong gulp of his.

"What do you suggest for damage control?"

Geoffrey faced the window and looked outside taking a moment to collect his thoughts. He took a sip of bourbon, turning to face Hendrick.

"Africa."

"Excuse me?"

"I've looked into some options and we need huge PR points right now. Not only that but Africa needs people to help build a school and a hospital in one of its most impoverished places."

"And this is going to work?"

"Brilliantly. We are going to give them a ton of money while you are going to fly there and get your hands dirty to show the world what your company really stands for."

"After this mess, it's the least I can do."

"Good, because you leave on Monday."

As Hendrick packed for his trip, he wondered what Africa was going to be like. He had never made a personal trip there and out of all the fundraisers and events none had ever supported Africa, so he had no need to visit there. He made sure to pack light fabrics due to the heat. It might actually be good to get out and work with people again one-on-one.

Lately, it seemed all he did was throw money around. He knew that wasn't always what it was all about. Despite the hard labor he was about to endure, he was looking forward to getting away from the politics of the company. He would also get away from the media.

As he lounged aboard his private jet heading to Africa, he reflected on the life he had led and how much he had in life. He was able to pick up and go on a whim because he didn't have any attachments. He was a 33-year-old man, never married or had children. Hell, he didn't even have a girlfriend. Even though he had, on occasion, taken a girl out for a night in town and then cooked her breakfast in the morning, he rarely ever saw the same person twice. He wasn't opposed to it, and he didn't view himself as a player, he was just busy and really bored. It had to take a special kind of lady to not only keep him on his toes, but to provide the kind of mental and physical stimulation he required to stick around. He had devoted his whole life to building the type of empire that would take care of him his entire life. He had no need to work a day in his life but he liked to keep busy and he was always in front of the media. He used to be the poster child for success and philanthropic acts until his company had been found out to be polluting the ocean.

He rubbed his hands through his hair in frustration. He would like to strangle the moron who made that decision, probably hoping Hendrick would never find out. Or maybe he thought Hendrick would applaud his genius. There are many fake philanthropists out there, but Hendrick wasn't one of them.

"Mr. Cooper, would you like another drink? We are about to serve your dinner."

"Yes, Amanda, that sounds wonderful. Make it a little stiffer though this time around."

She smiled at him a little too long and he could tell just by the look on her face that she would like something stiff as well. He wouldn't mind taking her into the back cabin and bending her over, but he had a strict rule against sleeping with staff. It was all trouble and he wanted no part of it. He certainly didn't need more bad press, especially if he happened to anger a female worker. Although it certainly depended on a case-by-case situation, he knew that most of the women that hit on him were looking to marry a handsome billionaire, and why not, right? What more could a girl ask for?

Although he was going to Africa to help out, he had sent over some luxuries to indulge in such as whiskey, cigars and chocolate. He sent a lot over in order to share; he wasn't greedy. He would be there for a few weeks at least and he wasn't giving up all the things he enjoyed in life.

His dinner was served and he downed the bourbon in one gulp. He delighted in his grilled salmon steak and asparagus. He enjoyed a healthy lifestyle and he happened to enjoy seafood of any kind. It was just as important in his success to keep his body as well as his mind clean and healthy. He decided to take a nap before the jet landed and his new adventure began.

Africa radiated with beauty in the same way that it radiated heat. He was in awe as soon as they arrived at the location in which he would be staying for the time period. He was staying in a cabin with a porch and although it wasn't luxurious, it was perfect for what he would need. He decided to unpack first before finding the man in charge. He noticed his packages had arrived including the wine that Geoffrey had sent in case Hendrick dined with any special guests. There were also pounds of individually wrapped chocolates that would be handed out to the children.

When he finished unpacking, he ventured out to his porch, plopping himself down on a wooden lounge chair. He looked around at all the lush greens of the forest, enamored that such places existed in the world. How lucky was he to be here and how lucky to be part of helping better a village. He noticed he had a hammock and looked forward to lounging in it at night. He had not been in a hammock since he was a kid. Both his parents died when he was 12 and he was raised for the most part by an aunt he was never close to. So again, attachments weren't really his thing.

He got up, grabbed a bottle of water and headed to the site. He wanted to talk to the head honcho and find out what the plan for the day would be. He had arranged, as well as paid for all the supplies that would be needed to build a new school and a hospital that the villagers desperately needed.

He was happy to have worn a hat because the African sun beat down hard. It wasn't overbearing though, and there was none of the humidity that he was used to in the summer months, so the heat there was dry so it didn't feel as hot.

When he arrived on location, the place was bustling with people. Some of the local villagers were around watching the goings on and getting a look at the new visitors. There were many volunteers sorting through supplies and they already had the frame of the school underway. He felt a sudden rush of pride at what he saw and what he was now a part of. The media could kiss his ass if they thought he could ever be involved in poisoning the earth.

"Mr. Cooper, welcome!"

Hendrick turned to find a very red-faced man standing behind him. His pale complexion was clearly not doing well in the sun, causing Hendrick to wonder why the skin wouldn't just tan instead of keeping a perpetual burn. He shook the sweaty palm of the pale fellow.

"It's a pleasure to have you here, sir, the supplies you sent were extremely generous. As you can see, the volunteers have already begun the project."

"Please call me Hendrick, there's no need for formalities here." He smiled warmly as the fella seemed nervous. "And you would be?"

"Oh my apologies, I'm Fred Cambridge, I am head of the project. Many projects actually. I've been here for over a year heading many projects for the corporation your company contacted."

"Perfect, well you're just the man I wanted to see then. What would you like me to help out with? And please I'm willing to help with any dirty work."

Fred chuckled, "Very good then, are you any good with a hammer?"

"I'm actually excellent with a hammer, just show me the way."

Hendrick felt a tugging on his leg and looked down to find a skinny little African girl tugging on the leg of his shorts.

“Well hello there.”

The girl smiled up at him with the most beautiful brown eyes he had ever seen.

“Many of the school children wander over during break. Their current school is falling apart and not nearly big enough for the number of children they have. So from time to time we may have some of the students visiting us.”

“Well I look forward to visiting with everyone.”

Fred walked Hendrick over to the group and introduced him. Hendrick could tell by the way they looked at him that they knew they had a billionaire amongst them. It was something he was used to at this point; he never quite got treated the same as everyone else. It was no big deal though, people warmed up to him eventually, once they got to know him and realized he wasn't a snobby prick. They got to work immediately and Hendrick felt a soul-cleansing feeling come over him from the hard work.

He hammered into those boards, letting out the pent-up aggression that he felt over the charges against his company. All his anger and pain went into the boards of that school building. By the end of the day they had a full frame completed on the school.

“Wow, it just looks fantastic everyone, good job.”

There were plenty of high fives and slaps on the back to go around. Hendrick was sweaty and tired, but he hadn’t felt that good in a really long time.

"I would very much like you all to join me at my cabin for dinner tonight. I'm having a fantastic dinner sent over and I want to share it with you all. You deserve it. And if that doesn't excite you I also have booze."

A cheer rang up around him and he laughed. "Ok I will see you in an hour, I'm sure you can find it."

A younger guy, not even 25, approached Hendrick; he thought maybe his name was Adam. "Hey, Hendrick. We have the volunteers at the school to have dinner with as well. Is it okay if I invite them as well?"

"Oh hell ya, of course. The more the merrier."

Adam grinned, "Thanks, man, you're pretty cool."

Hendrick laughed, "Ya I get that sometimes."

Chapter Two

Hendrick had a table set up outside of his cabin, and food had been brought in from the nearest town. Everyone showed up right on time, introductions followed one by one of the volunteers from the school.

There was one woman, he couldn't tell her age, but she had creamy brown skin the color of dark brown sugar with a smile that quite literally lit up the room. He had watched her walk up to his cabin with a few friends, chatting amiably. She stood tall and thin and had the athletic build of a professional dancer. Her eyes were big, round and the color of chestnuts. He could not take his eyes off of her; she was absolutely stunning. Stunning, yet all she wore were cargo shorts and a plain white volunteer t-shirt. She was checking out the food table; it was divine and the volunteers probably hadn't had food like that since they got there.

He made a beeline for her and almost knocked another volunteer over in the process. "I'm sorry," he muttered as he walked by.

Hendrick approached her group as they gathered some food.

"Hello, can I get you guys something to drink?"

She looked up then, meeting his eyes and it was like a gift. He didn't know what the hell was wrong with him because he certainly never went all gooey with any other woman he had been interested in. She smiled very naturally at him and said, "Hi, Mr. Cooper, is it? I'm Jocelyn, I'm one of the AIDS volunteers here."

"Jocelyn, what a beautiful name, and please call me Hendrick."

She blushed at the compliment, pleasing him more.

"Hendrick it is then. Thank you for the invite, we were famished and this looks wonderful."

"You're welcome. I also sent food to the village to help out."

"Oh, well that's very kind of you. I'm sure it's greatly appreciated."

"Well it's nothing for me to do it, so I feel it's my duty."

She stared at him, almost seeing him for the first time. They shook hands and he held hers just a bit too long. So long in fact one of her friends started to giggle.

Composing himself quickly, Hendrick got a drink order from them. He poured Jocelyn and her two friends a glass of wine each and brought it back to them. He didn't want to overstay his welcome with the group. So he handed them their glasses, leaving them to eat. He headed to the table, grabbed a plate full of food and went to sit with Fred. Fred chatted easily with Hendrick as they ate. Hendrick found he didn't have much to say. The food was delicious, chicken and ribs with vegetables and potatoes. Fresh vegetables and fruit came with the food as well and it was a delectable meal. He found that although it was delicious, he couldn't focus on it much because he kept glancing at Jocelyn. He wanted her, he wanted her more than anything and he was determined to have her. She was easily the most beautiful creature he had even seen; he knew she would be his.

He watched her throughout the night and became more infatuated with her. The best part about it was that she glanced his way on occasion as well, and he could swear that it made him semi-hard every time she did it.

He looked over at Fred who was sipping a bourbon rather happily. "How well do you know the volunteers at the school?"

"Oh quite well. I'm always introduced to new volunteers and they visit our camps regularly."

"What is Jocelyn's story?"

Fred chuckled, "Ah interested in the girl are you? She is beautiful to be sure but she hasn't shown interest in anyone outside of her camp since she's been here. She seems very private."

Hendrick nodded. "She really isn't a girl is she?"

Fred laughed loudly bringing attention to them. Jocelyn met his eyes again, holding them for a beat. Fred carried on, "No, she's 26, I believe, and incredibly smart. I think she is here on a whim to escape her life temporarily. But I guess that's really why we are all here isn't it, Hendrick?"

Hendrick met his gaze and knew that Fred had heard about the trouble with his company. He hoped he didn't think negatively about him; he didn't want anyone to believe the nonsense rumors about him.

"Yes, I'm afraid that's usually the case."

As people started filtering out of the area and returning to their own lodgings, Hendrick boldly went over to Jocelyn and asked if she would stick around and have another drink with him. Her friend giggled again, walking away.

"Sure, I would love that. I can't stay late though. The mornings are far too early for me." She laughed gently and he enjoyed the sound of it.

They walked back up to the porch and Jocelyn sat down on a chair while Hendrick made them a stiff drink. She had been drinking wine all night but he didn't think she would be opposed to liquor. He headed back to the porch and handed her the glass. She didn't miss a beat, taking a sip of her drink. He sat down beside her and they sat in silence for a moment looking out into the lush greens as the sun began to set.

"So tell me Jocelyn, what exactly does your volunteer team do here in regards to the AIDS movement?"

"It's education-based, that's why we are at the schools. We are trying to teach them about the disease and most importantly how to prevent it. It's so rampant here that all we can do is tell them how to avoid it."

"You're pretty young to be doing something like this, aren't you?"

She laughed, "I'm not that young." She stared at him long enough to make the statement hold some power.

"I suppose not, but shouldn't someone of your age be partying and out having some fun."

"Well I certainly did a lot of that when I hit my twenties but I can't say that I'm much for clubbing."

He nodded watching her.

"So what made you come here?"

She turned to face him, "You first. You're quite wealthy, why come down here yourself?"

"Well something happened in my life recently that caused me a bit of trouble. This is my escape, and not only that but it was time I got back into the nitty-gritty. When I was younger I did missions all the time. It's easy to throw money at a situation, but far harder to come down and meet it face-to-face."

"I totally know what you mean. Well not totally," she laughed. "Not the billions."

"So, your turn."

"I came down because my life was too easy and I felt guilty." She looked into her hands unable to meet his gaze any longer.

"Hmmm. I think you're going to have to explain that one."

She looked at him wistfully and took a deep breath. "Well I don't have a terrible back story. And you would be surprised how many people look at me and expect me to have an incredible journey attached to my success and I don't."

"What kind of story should you have?"

"I'm not explaining myself very well here, am I?"

He chuckled, "No worries, please explain."

"Well I'm not from the projects. My family is normal and educated. There are no drunks or crime in our family. I led a normal life and I ended up going to University for fashion and once I graduated, my father lent me the money to start my own design business. Although I'm not rich and famous yet, my company does turn a decent profit."

"That's something to be proud of, Jocelyn. So how does the guilt fit into this?"

"You are so easy to talk to, I hadn't expected that." They smiled at each other and he couldn't have felt happier that he caused her comfort.

"Hold that thought, while I grab us another drink." Hendrick quickly went in and poured them a short drink. It was getting late and he didn't want her to feel hung-over in the morning. He returned, handing her the glass.

"Please tell me why you feel guilty about your success."

"Well I met a girl in University who did have a tragic upbringing and she fought to get through school and she did her thesis paper on the history of the African-Americans and so on."

She paused and he waited her out. He sipped his drink, completely mesmerized by this girl.

"My friend made me feel guilty I guess. We still remained close after University and she went into politics and I went into fashion. One day she showed me this video about things going on in the world. She implored me to start helping out and suddenly I looked at my life seeing all that I had. I just felt it, ya know? Felt that I too needed to give back because I had been so lucky. So I put my sister in-charge of my company temporarily and I came here. I plan on being here for a month and I'm almost done, so I'm doing the best that I can with the time I have."

"Wow, I don't even know you Jocelyn and I'm incredibly proud of you. Your parents must have been thrilled."

She laughed, "Actually they weren't. They felt they had worked really hard to give me a better life, a different life than they had growing up. They wanted me to reap the benefits of it, not immerse myself into the very life they had wanted me to avoid."

"They will come around. Parents always want the best for their kids and it's usually what they want for themselves more. You did something great, it's only temporary and then you will be back making dresses in no time."

"Thank you, Hendrick, I appreciate you saying that."

"Oh, you know I'm wise beyond my years," he joked trying to make light of their talk.

"Oh you can't be that much older than me."

"I'm a bit, I'll be turning 34 in six months. I have lots of experience."

"Experience in what?" she whispered. And it was the way she whispered that caught him off guard. It was almost like she was breathless.

He couldn't find any words to answer her and he felt like he was losing a handle on things.

"I like you, Hendrick, I feel like you understand me."

"I like you too, Jocelyn, a little too much for my own good."

"Well we can't be good all the time, can we?"

He just stared at her. Her brown eyes bore into his. He wanted to ravish her right then but he didn't know if he should make a move. They had just met and he didn't want to start something he couldn't finish. They would be working together now and he didn't want to make things worse. However, there was the problem of how he could only think of sliding inside her and seeing what she felt like wrapped around him.

She got up then and made the decision for him. She bore her mouth onto his and the fire that lit between them was intense. She gasped inside his mouth and his loins burned for her. His hands went into her hair, pulling her closer to him. He kissed her deeply finding her tongue and sucking on it gently. She moaned and the sounds she made caused him to go rock hard. Oh yes, he would have her tonight. He needed to hear her moan all night long.

He stood up then and pulled her body to his. He kissed down to her chin and trailed kisses down her neck sucking on her. Her hands found the bulge in his shorts, rubbing him hard causing a friction that drove him insane. The knowledge that she was eager for his cock drove him half mad. He picked her up, carrying her into the cabin and laid her out on his bed. He pulled off her t-shirt and unclasped her bra. Her breasts dropped deliciously from the bra and he bent down to suck on her dark nipples. She gave a guttural moan and he sucked even harder. She pushed him away, tearing off her shorts and he glimpsed a pair of white lace panties before she slid them to the floor.

He dropped to the floor in front of her, spreading her legs as she leaned back. Her pussy was so pink it made him crazy. She was already wet and he slid a finger inside her, feeling her drip down his finger. She moaned his name and it was just about the best sound he had ever heard. He leaned in and sucked her clit forcing her to thrash beneath him. He sucked her good while fucking her with his finger. She came all over his finger and he pulled out.

"Please, Hendrick, I want you inside me."

He never wanted a lady to beg; he would give her exactly what she wanted. He pulled her up and turned her over. She gasped in excitement as she bent over for him, her tight round bottom in his face. He bent down and kissed her bottom, moving in real close to her. He was rock hard and he couldn't wait to plunge inside her pink little pussy. Her tight bottom drove him insane and he drove deep inside her causing her to moan loudly. She was tight and wet and he really had to control himself or he would lose himself completely inside her.

"Hendrick, I need it."

Her ass looked glorious right before him as he plunged deeper inside and moved within her. She called out to him loudly and he briefly wondered if there was anyone within earshot. He could have cared less however; let the whole village hear. He was fucking an amazing woman and he wouldn't stop for anything.

She came against his cock and he continued to rock inside her until he spilled into her as well. He leaned down on top of her back, breathing heavily into her hair.

"Oh Jocelyn, that was incredible."

"You bet your ass it was," and she giggled underneath him. He rolled off of her and lay down on the bed. She lay beside him and they were silent thinking about what had just happened between them. She rolled into his chest and nuzzled into it. He wrapped his hands around her and kissed her on the top of the head.

"Yes that definitely was amazing." They fell asleep tangled up in each other's arms.

Chapter Three

When Hendrick awoke that morning, he felt glorious. He had slept like the dead and despite the hard labor of the day before, he awoke completely rested, ready to start the day. He rolled over to kiss Jocelyn good morning and realized he was in the bed alone. She must have woken before him, dressed and left while he slept. He hadn't even heard her leave. He suddenly worried that she might be upset.

He washed up in the basin left out for him and dressed quickly. He was determined to talk to Jocelyn before he began the work for the day. But when he arrived at the old school she was nowhere to be found. He asked her friends if they had seen her and although they both had a mischievous glint in their eyes, they claimed that neither had seen her that morning. He was starting to run late so he headed to his camp, knowing he would have to try to meet up with her later.

The sun beat down heavy on them that day and although they accomplished a lot by lunch, he was utterly exhausted from the heat. He would have given anything for a cold shower at that point.

Instead of heading with the crowd to find lunch, he grabbed a bottle of water and headed to the school. He had not been able to stop thinking about Jocelyn all morning. It was very unlike him; usually he could forget a girl he slept with by lunch. Jocelyn was different however; she intrigued him. He saw her when he entered the school yard, she was with the children playing outside.

He walked right up to her and she smiled when she saw him. "Hendrick, I didn't expect you, welcome to the school."

She didn't appear uncomfortable or awkward at all.

"Can we talk?"

Surprise crossed her face and she looked around at the children. "Why don't you guys go back inside so we can begin the lesson?"

"Take these with you." He handed the children a handful of chocolates. They ran inside excitedly ripping them open as they ran.

Jocelyn laughed as they ran away. "Well that sure worked."

He watched her, "You left this morning."

"Yes. Did that bother you?"

"No. I just wanted to make sure you weren't upset about what happened last night."

"How could I be upset, you made me feel quite good."

She had a glint in her eye that made him envision a teacher's desk and her bent over it.

"Well good, I'm glad. I don't want you to be."

"I wasn't sure if it would have been weird for you to wake up beside me, so I got up. I needed to get ready for work anyways."

"I would like the chance to wake up beside you if you allow me to."

"Oh my, Hendrick, what are you suggesting?"

"I'm suggesting you allow me to touch your body anytime I want to."

She gasped. But she didn't say no.

A week passed and Jocelyn was over every night. He filled her with his cock every night. She was a drug to him and he could not get enough of her. The second night they were together, he put his cock in her mouth and she did things to it that made him see heaven early. All he did was fuck her in every position he could imagine; he needed to have her over and over again. He was insatiable when he was around her. He couldn't even have a peaceful dinner with her without needing his dessert first; only then could they sit and enjoy a meal.

New volunteers had arrived and the school was almost finished. They had a rather large team at this point, so work finished quickly. Next they would begin the hospital and then who knows? Geoffrey was showing up that day to give him an update on the company. He didn't have his phone with him; it would have been far too distracting so he had left it at home. So that meant Geoffrey travelling to Africa to bring Hendrick any news.

When Geoffrey arrived, Hendrick was having lunch with Jocelyn at her camp. It took Geoffrey awhile to find Hendrick and he was drenched in sweat when he finally did.

"Holy it's hot here."

Hendrick laughed, "Well you get used to it."

Hendrick introduced Geoffrey to Jocelyn and he could tell that Geoffrey liked her immediately.

"I have an update for you on the issue, if we could talk in private."

"Ya let's do that." He looked at Jocelyn and she had a puzzled look on her face.

"I will see you later, okay?"

She nodded, not saying a word. Hendrick thought her behavior was a little weird, but he quickly forgot it when he walked away with Geoffrey.

"So what's the word, my good man?"

"You look really good, Hendrick, nice and relaxed, good for you."

"Thanks to you. This was a great idea, I needed to get away from all the stress of being accused of poisoning the ocean."

"I know, believe me we are going to walk away from this."

"Good, so what's the word?"

"You need to be finished here in a few weeks whether the hospital is complete or not because you are to appear in front of the court for the criminal charges brought against you."

"I'm not going to jail because the Arctic Ocean was poisoned."

"You aren't, Hendrick, it's all going to go away, swept under the rug and everyone will be back to thinking you are as amazing as always."

"Awesome, that's what I like to hear."

They continued walking to the camp so that Hendrick could show him the progress of the project but neither of them had noticed the person walking behind them the whole time.

Chapter Four

When Jocelyn didn't show up at his cabin for dinner that night, Hendrick grew worried and went out to look for her. He didn't have to look far, however, as she had never left her own camp the whole night. He found her out on the grass of her own cabin. She didn't even look up at him as he approached.

"Hey, what happened to you tonight? I thought you were coming over?"

"Well I guess you thought wrong, Hendrick."

Shocked, he didn't know how to respond, she sounded so cold.

"Is something wrong? Have I done something to upset you?"

She finally looked up at him and just glared. He couldn't have been more confused at that moment. He didn't know what to say to her, so he said nothing. Girls usually spoke again anyways; they were always so inclined to make sure their word was spoken and no man would be getting the upper hand on them.

She was still staring at him and he could swear she bore a hole right through him.

"You poisoned that ocean. You came down here and you're nothing but a fake."

He was so taken aback that he didn't know how to respond, which made him look completely guilty.

"Why would you say that to me?"

"I heard you and your friend talking today. You guys were so immersed in your evil that you didn't even notice I was right behind you."

"No, Jocelyn, you don't understand. I mean yes what you heard was correct, but I had nothing to do with it."

"Oh well how convenient for you. It's not like we haven't heard that story before. Something dirty goes on in a company and the owner just has no idea, right?"

"I assure you, Jocelyn, I had no idea, I'm rarely even at the company anymore."

"That doesn't mean you don't know what's going on there. Like who really has no idea what their own company is doing in regards to waste management?"

He couldn't even believe what he was hearing. He had said the very same thing before heading to Africa. And now Jocelyn didn't believe a word he said.

"I know it sounds crazy, but it's true. Even Geoffrey had no idea. I am going to court but it doesn't mean I did it. I'm defending myself, I had no idea that this was something that was going on at my company and the prosecutor can't prove otherwise."

"It's completely disgusting what happened and I just have a hard time believing you had nothing to do with it."

"Please, Jocelyn. I have spent my whole life trying to do right by people. You know me, really you already know me so well. I would never do something so careless and stupid, I'm trying to better the world, not ruin it."

"Are you here to run away from the press?"

"No, the complete opposite actually. I want them to see who I really am and then judge my character. I've only been here a week and I am so much happier than I have been in years."

She looked at him deep in the eyes and seemingly searched for answers. He didn't know what he could do that would make her believe him. He felt like she should already know his character.

"Please come back to my cabin with me. Being near you is driving me crazy."

"Please don't lie to me."

"I would never. I'm telling you the truth, please believe me."

She leaned into him and kissed him roughly. It excited him and he started undressing her right then. He knew she shared a cabin with the two other girls from the school but he didn't care.

"Hendrick, we can't."

"Shhh, we'll be quiet, I'm not waiting."

They quickly undressed each other and he lay her down in the grass, spreading her legs wide. He liked looking at her pink pussy, it drove him insane with lust. Her opening was always wet and ready for him. He slid a finger inside her and rocked her gently. She was holding back her cries. He got his finger very wet from her pussy and slowly inserted it into her bum being careful that he was gentle. She couldn't hold back; she cried out in pleasure and he inserted his finger repeatedly. He loved looking at her in the throes of passion.

He took his finger out and climbed on top of her, pushing his cock inside. He pumped inside her hard and she fought back the moans she so desperately wanted to scream out. He had her alright and he made her come over and over again as he fucked her with an intensity she would not soon forget. He finally spilled into her and they lay together in the grass, spent. He rolled over to her and kissed her deeply on the mouth.

"You have completely bewitched me, Jocelyn, whatever am I going to do with you?"

"Anything you want, Hendrick, anything you want."

He had returned that night to his own bed though he wished that she had went with him. He could still remember the feeling of being inside her and he wanted to do it all over again before he went to bed. He would have to wait another evening however. He fell asleep as soon as his head hit the pillow.

When the sun hit his eyes that morning he opened them to find Jocelyn already there with two cups of coffee in her hands. He rubbed at his eyes sure that it was a dream.

"What are you doing here? Why didn't you just come back with me last night?"

"I was torn, I'm sorry. I have something to tell you."

"What is it?"

"I'm leaving today."

He sat right up in bed and said, "What?"

"I'm sorry, I should have told you sooner but I didn't want to make a big thing of it. I just wanted to enjoy my time with you and then go. My time serving here is over. I've already been gone a month and my sister needs me to take my company off her hands. I have to go."

"I can't believe you're going. What am I going to do here without you?"

She laughed, "Work, I suppose. I really enjoyed our time together Hendrick but I need to get back to my life and move on. I hope you understand."

He didn't of course, but he refused to let her see that he was devastated. There was nothing he could do about her sudden departure so it was best he let her go and figure out a way to deal with it later.

"Sure. I wish you well with your company."

A sad look came over her and she leaned in to kiss him.

"Take care, Hendrick."

And with that he watched her walk out of his cabin and into the lush green of the forest around them.

-To be continued in Book 2-

If you enjoyed this title, I would appreciate your leaving a review of the book. Good reviews encourage an author to write as well as help books to sell. Good reviews can be just a few short sentences describing what you liked about the book without having a spoiler. If you could spend 30 seconds writing a review, I would appreciate it: you can review this title right now at your favorite retailer.

Here is a preview of the **next book** you may also enjoy:

Love Belated - Elusive Billionaire Romance Series, Book 2

JOCELYN WAS rushing around like a chicken with her head cut off. To say she was stressed out would be an understatement. She hurried into the cafe around the corner from her studio and grabbed coffee as well as the most delicious donuts for her whole team. She put in her order and tried with all her might to be patient while it was made. She had a huge deadline due that day to provide sketches for a well-known female rock star for an upcoming awards show and she needed everything to go fabulously. She needed this job to bring her career to the next level.

She had been working like a well-trained poodle since she came back from Africa six months prior. She wanted to start making things happen in her life just as she had always imagined. Or maybe it had a lot to do with the man she had left in Africa. She had not spoken to Hendrick since she left and she knew it was the best thing. The man was trouble. It had been a short little fling that she was determined to keep in her past and that was that. She had to question her drive lately and how much that had to do with the fact that she was trying to forget feelings that she had begun to develop with Hendrick. What a fool. What, you fell in love after a few weeks? She wasn't about to believe that and she certainly wasn't going to tie herself pathetically to a man that had never had a serious relationship in his entire life. No, thank you.

So she dove into her work with great gusto in the hopes that she could forget the way in which he ignited her body every time he touched her. It had been good for her though; the work she had put into her company in the past six months had made it grow significantly. Now she had a team behind her that worked with her in creating her designs. She used to do all the sewing herself and getting everything ready for shows, and now she was able to delegate those tasks to someone else. It was the most empowering and liberating feeling to be in her position. But it also meant she stood in a coffee line stressed to the nines waiting for a beverage. Man, if she could just get this songstress to wear her designs she would be laughing. The girl could virtually wear garbage bags and people went nuts, so having her wear her own designs would definitely benefit her greatly.

Coffee trays in hand, she headed for the door. Her team deserved frequent coffee fixes, they had worked so hard, so it was the least she could do for them. Plus in general, she just enjoyed making people happy. When she stepped out into the sun and headed towards her studio, she stopped abruptly in the middle of the sidewalk. Screw it, she thought, I'm taking a moment. She stood there on the sidewalk and just pointed her face toward the sky and took a deep relaxing breath. She loved her life and all the great things she had. She was blessed in so many ways and she had no reason to be stressed. With so many people dying in the world, her designs were hardly anything to worry about. And what's more, she was genuinely happy and delighted for her future.

She walked the rest of the way to her office with a new lightness of foot. When she walked into the open concept room, one of her girls ran over and grabbed one of the trays out of her hands.

"Oh thank you. I was so worried I was going to spill coffee and donuts on my way over here."

The girl's name was Samantha and she was Jocelyn's right hand lady. Samantha laughed as she helped Jocelyn with passing out the coffee.

"You got a package today, it looks sort of luxurious."

Jocelyn laughed, "Really? Maybe little miss rock star is trying to bribe my designs in early."

"You don't know who it's from?"

"I couldn't even imagine."

Samantha followed Jocelyn over to her desk and they both stared down at the box. It certainly was an expensively wrapped package and staring at it puzzled Jocelyn further.

"I don't know Jose, it sort of looks romantic."

"Romantic?" Jocelyn laughed and with that she quickly opened the package to find a stunning red dress inside with a necklace that screamed big dollars.

"Oh my god."

"There's a letter, open it!" Samantha practically yelled.

"Okay, okay, I will."

She picked up the letter and turned it over; there was no name or address on it. She opened it and there in simple words was a message to meet at Le Amore, the fanciest restaurant in town. She was to wear the elegant items in the box.

"Who on earth...?"

If you enjoyed this sample then look for **Love Belated - Elusive Billionaire Romance Series, Book 2**.

Here is a preview of **another book** you may also enjoy:

Love Eluded - Audacious Billionaire BWWM Romance Series, Book 1

CHANTE GREEN knew she was going to be late for work…again.

"Shit…," she mumbled, impatiently tapping her foot as she craned her neck to see if the bus was anywhere in sight.

She could almost see the look of annoyance on the face of her supervisor, Nurse Betty Lebowitz. It was the third time this month alone and Chante knew she was hanging by a thread. She could lose her job at New York General Hospital, and she needed that now more than ever.

Chante genuinely hoped that Nurse Betty would be a little sympathetic and cut her some slack. After all, the supervisor was familiar with the reason Chante was under a tremendous amount of pressure. Her brother Markey had ALS or Amyotrophic Lateral Sclerosis, also known as Lou Gehrig's disease.

A catastrophic disease that was initially misdiagnosed, Markey now had only partial control of his legs. Looking back, he was always clumsy as a child, often falling or stumbling, but everyone said it was just a phase and he'll eventually outgrow it. But as the years progressed, Chante noticed the slurred speech. Her mom eventually took him to a specialist who, after rigorous testing declared the boy was in the second stages of ALS.

Things became even more difficult when Chante's dad contracted malaria and eventually died from it. Chante and her mom, both heartbroken over the sudden death, struggled to meet the special needs that were required to deal with ALS. Her mom, having had experience in caring for sick children, took on most of the responsibilities. When swallowing became too hard, they took turns giving him food through a feeding tube. Mom would bathe him; help him use the bathroom; exercise his arms and legs to prevent atrophy, until her son's disease took its toll on her as well.

Driving one night to buy medicine at a nearby pharmacy, she was too preoccupied to notice the red light at a street intersection and was hit on the driver's side by a passing truck. She was in a coma for three days before she succumbed to her injuries. At nineteen years old, Chante was left with an enormous responsibility towards a brother who was not even of her own blood, but who meant more to her than anything in the whole world. He was her only family.

Chante didn't remember much of her early childhood years, except shuttling from one foster home to another. At six years old, she was considered too old by most couples wanting to adopt a baby. The shy and gawky black girl with soulful green eyes was never chosen. Unable to find a good family for her, city officials decided to turn her over to the State Institution for Unwanted Children. On the eve of her departure, a woman came in, noticed her cringing in a corner, and approached her.

Chante believed she was an angel with blond hair falling softly around her shoulder. But it was the sweet voice that calmed her enough to reach for the hand that was offered to her. The woman was enamored with the emaciated child and decided to adopt her. The lady, Hannah Green, brought her home and introduced her to her husband, Caleb, a Mulatto who was delighted to see her. Chante felt an instant kinship with the dark-skinned stranger. Hannah made her feel like the daughter they never had. Both were missionaries who went to far-flung places on medical missions.

Chante spent her growing years travelling to places most children would have found depressing. No electricity, no running water, and sometimes just a hut to sleep on at night, if they were lucky. Otherwise, it had to be in a tent or under the stars. Children with malaria, TB, pneumonia, measles, and countless other maladies constantly filled their days.

From her adoptive parents, Chante learned compassion, dedication, and sympathy for the sick. No one was turned away. There was always room for one more.

Chante blossomed under their care. The lost look in her eyes gradually changed to confidence. She learned her ABC's under Acacia trees with other children. Instead of children's books, medical books were her constant companion. She couldn't read most of the words, but the pictures amazed her. It was no surprise that she declared she would become a doctor someday. She changed her mind after she found her passion working alongside the nurses, who took care of their patients day in and day-out.

It was during one of these missions that her mom and dad discovered that they were expecting a baby. Chante's innate insecurity returned. She knew she was adopted and was afraid to be given away again. Her parents, seeing the troubled look on her face, assured her that she would always be a part of their family. They loved her so much like she was their very own, they said. That restored her confidence so much so that when the baby finally arrived, Chante immediately fell in love with the little bundle of crinkly skin and puffy eyes. No one seeing them for the first time would ever doubt they were brother and sister. They looked so much alike… same curly hair and bronzed chocolaty skin complexion.

When Chante's dad contracted malaria and eventually died from it, they moved to a smaller house. Maintaining the big sprawling colonial house where Chante grew up became too much for her mom. Money was scarce with the little pension she was receiving from her work as a missionary and Chante was in her last year in high school.

If you enjoyed this sample then look for **Love Eluded - Audacious Billionaire BWWM Romance Series, Book 1**.

Here is a preview of **another book** you may also enjoy:

Love Invested – Persuasive Billionaire BWWM Romance Series, Book 1

"**THEY'RE ASKING** for the eggs to be cooked again."

"What? Those are fine!"

"What do you want me to do about it, Brad? The customer is complaining. Just make them again, alright? He wants the eggs overcooked, apparently."

Brad took the plate from Stacey's hand and returned to his grill, grumbling loudly. Stacey wiped the sweat from her brow and turned around, getting ready to head back out onto the floor of *Papa's Grill and Diner*.

It was the middle of the day in mid-summer, which made the sweltering kitchen unbearable. Stacey was glad to leave the kitchen even if it meant dealing with a couple of jerk customers.

Back in the dining area, she looked around. She had only one couple in her section. They were older, with their shoulders hunched over and beady eyes pointed toward the kitchen. The woman hadn't touched her sandwich, probably waiting for the man to get his eggs back before digging in.

There was only one other waitress, Maria, working, and she was in the corner, texting on her phone. Their place wasn't exactly the hot spot of the city to eat during the best of times. During mid-day, it was more like a graveyard.

The woman motioned for Stacey to come over. She clenched her jaw, exhaled slowly and got ready for whatever ridiculous request the woman was going to make. This couple had been a hassle from the moment they were seated.

"How can I help you?" she asked, plastering a smile on her face.

The woman scowled, "Where are my husband's eggs?"

"They're making him a fresh batch right now."

"Tell them to hurry up!" the woman snapped.

The husband sat there silently, playing with the edge of his napkin. But he nodded at Stacey as if to tell her he better get his eggs soon.

Stacey scurried back into the kitchen. It was mind-numbing if she let it get to her. How long had she been working here now? Four years? It was supposed to be a pit stop before she moved onto bigger and better things. She had been there, scraping by, instead of returning to college or working on making something more of herself.

No use in thinking about that now.

Brad handed her a plate of freshly cooked eggs. She walked back to the table and placed it in front of the man and his wife.

The man wrinkled his nose and said, "This will do, I suppose."

Stacey clasped her hands together and inquired as politely as she could muster, "Would you like more coffee?"

They grunted, and she gave them a fresh pot, making sure not to add it their bill. She was sure they would want something for free out of the egg fiasco. By the time the couple left, Stacey was ready for a break.

In the break room, she slipped off her shoes and rubbed her feet, wincing. Her shoes were cheap, and it showed after standing in them for more than a couple of hours. Her feet were killing her.

She checked her phone next. There was a voicemail from her sister. It was a rare event that her sister reached out to her and she was filled with dread listening to the message.

"Stacey, hey. It's your sister, Allison," she added for clarification as if Stacey wouldn't know her own sister's name. "Listen, call me when you can? I have a question to ask you. Well, more of a favor? But I need to talk to you first. Thanks, bye."

Stacey sighed as the message ended. Her sister wanting a favor never led to anything good. *If she wants money, she can forget it.* There was no cash to give Allison. There were barely any funds for Stacey.

A small TV in the break room played the news. The image was grainy but she could just make out the weatherman talking about rain later on in the evening. *Great.* She made a mental note to make sure the roof didn't leak all over everything when she got home from work. Last time it stormed, Stacey had to set out buckets to catch the drips.

She closed her eyes just for a moment. If she left them closed for too long, she would fall asleep on the spot. It felt as if there was always something to do. She finished one thing, and another task popped up in its place. Maybe that was how it would always be.

"Wake up, sleepyhead."

Stacey opened her eyes to see Amanda stepping into the break room.

"You work today?" Stacey asked, surprised, wondering why they needed another waitress working during such a slow day.

"Nah, I left my wallet here last night in my locker. I was so tired after closing, it just slipped my mind." Amanda walked over to her locker and glanced back at Stacey. "You okay?"

"Yeah, just tired."

"Looks dead here. I'd be tired too," Amanda remarked as she opened up her locker.

"Yeah, it's pretty boring."

Amanda paused in front of her open locker, grabbed her wallet, and tucked it into her purse. When she turned back around, she had a strange look on her face. Stacey sat up straighter.

"What?"

Amanda hesitated and then sat down on the wooden bench. Stacey could see the purple circles under Amanda's eyes. Although they both worked full time at the restaurant, Amanda also attended college. She was probably just as tired as Stacey.

"I heard something. Probably just a rumor. I don't know. I wasn't going to tell anyone but—"

But I know how much you need this job was the unfinished thought there.

"What is it?"

Amanda lowered her voice, "Heard at a class yesterday this place might close down."

"Who was talking about that in your class?" Stacey scoffed. "Especially about our little place."

"Well, I mentioned that I work here. I was in my accounting class, and we were doing a project. This kid in my group said that I should look for other work because this place is going to shut down. Especially with all those investment groups coming in here trying to revive the area."

Stacey scowled. Her neighborhood, which was predominantly black, had indeed been crawling with rich white men in suits lately. All of them wanted to knock down and rebuild her section of town. They wanted to make it new and fresh again. They wanted it to appeal to the elite, which naturally meant getting rid of anyone who was low income.

"Thanks for the heads up, Amanda, but one kid in a college class saying we're going to close doesn't mean we are going to."

"Maybe. But this place is always dead. How long do you think we can stay open like this?" She stood up. "Don't tell anyone I told you, okay? I'll see you later."

Stacey watched her go, suddenly feeling wide awake. Even though she had sounded confident to Amanda that they weren't going to close, the girl had a point. Business had been awful lately. How long would they really be able to stay open?

Maybe it was time to find another job. The only reason Stacey had stuck around there for so long was how flexible the hours were. Few places would accommodate Stacey like that. But if this place was going to close, she may have to put some applications out.

She sighed and rubbed her forehead, fending off a headache. Just another worry to add to her long list.

If you enjoyed this sample then look for **Love Invested – Persuasive Billionaire BWWM Romance Series, Book 1**.

Other Books by Shyla Starr

- Persuasive Billionaire BWWM Romance Series

- Tenacious Billionaire BWWM Romance Series

- Lonely Billionaire Romance Series

- Ardent Billionaire Romance Series

- Fervent Billionaire BWWM Romance Series

- Audacious Billionaire BWWM Romance Series

Get the latest update on new releases from the author at:

https://shylastarr.com/newsletter/

About the Author - Shyla Starr

Shyla currently specializes in writing interracial romance stories and is a huge fan of the alpha male. Simply put, there just aren't enough stories about mixed couple romances, which is something she is aiming to fix.

Being a bookworm all her life, when Shyla discovered men she also realized how easy it was to fulfill her fantasies through her writing.

When not writing and fantasizing about men, Shyla enjoys dancing, reading and chilling with her friends.

Connect with Shyla Starr

I really appreciate you reading my book! Here are my social media coordinates:

Friend me on Facebook:
https://www.facebook.com/shylastarrauthor

Follow me on Twitter: https://twitter.com/shylstarr

Check me out on Goodreads:
https://www.goodreads.com/author/show/8436084.Shyla_Starr

Subscribe to my newsletter:
https://shylastarr.com/newsletter/

Visit my website: https://shylastarr.com/

www.ingramcontent.com/pod-product-compliance
Lightning Source LLC
Chambersburg PA
CBHW031631200726
48288CB00019B/1381